Animals in the Forest

The Day Terrible Things Came

A story to save the Earth

Kathryn Rose Newey

Dedicated to all animals on Earth – especially the ones we keep in cages, the ones we neglect and are cruel towards, and the wild ones trying to survive in disappearing habitats.

We are sorry.

<u>Table of Contents</u>

~ Chapter 1: A New Friend ~

The crow, who many would say was a bossy, noisy and clever bird (some even adding that he had the blackest and shiniest feathers of all birds), was often to be seen right at the very tops of trees, where he would sit and look for miles across the countryside.

This morning the crow had woken as usual and flown to a good surveying spot up high. Despite the light rain that was falling softly, like grasses waving in the breeze, the crow could see everything, near and far.

Just below him was the little forest grove, shaped like a green kidney in the landscape, where his animal acquaintances lived. If the crow looked really carefully, he could make out some small, indistinct shapes of some of his animal acquaintances moving in between the trees beneath him.

As he looked just beyond that, to the left of this landscape was the wide and long strip of road which carried fast moving human vehicles, endlessly reverberating with speed and sound. To the right and ahead, he could see gold and green planted fields and meadows stretching as far as his eyes could see, with more little woodlands and forest copses sticking up every now and then, like green caterpillars on a giant leaf.

A little away from this forest grove, and to the right, leading from a twisting track that came up to the forest, were the farm buildings which the humans occupied.

Between the farm buildings and the forest there was a small lake, which, when seen from this height, perfectly mirrored the sky - so a miniature sky, complete with grey clouds and some blue patches, appeared on the lake's surface. This little lake was connected to a gentle trickle of a brook, which meandered, on the far side, through the fields to join a small river beyond the farm buildings.

The crow knew this had all once looked very different, with many more forests, trees, birds and animals everywhere, and certainly fewer roads, machines and humans: but that was a long time ago. He knew this, because this information had been passed down through generations of crows over the centuries.

But despite this, and even though he had to fluff his black feathers to stop the rain dripping in, the crow felt a sense of satisfaction when he looked around this vast kingdom today. It seemed so peaceful, plentiful and beautiful.

But not for long. As he watched, some machines and humans stirred and rumbled and quaked into the farmyard. The soft rain made the farmyard activity look slightly blurry, but the vibrations were unmistakable, shaking the ground and undulating up the tree he was sitting in.

He watched the human activity with some interest. However from his high post, he couldn't discern anything out of the ordinary, except that even from afar, the machines did look different and seemed somewhat larger than he was used to.

Now, some would have said that this was a sign.

But the crow wasn't overly worried, because he knew the humans often carried out strange and noisy activities in the fields and farmyard and on the roads.

So, despite his ever watchful eyes, even he didn't sense the coming tragedy to this little piece of paradise.

~~~~~~~~~

Far below, as the clouds broke, some early morning sunlight reached soft, tentacle fingers into the gaps between the trees. It started warming up these little patches very slowly, and the glowing light gently woke up the animals who lived there. They stretched and yawned, shook off any water droplets, and got busy with daily living.

Dakota the Deer, who had only just woken up with the other deer, stopped in one of these patches in the woods, which was dappled with dots of sunshine. The sunlight created spots on
~~~~~~~~~

her soft red-brown fur, as if, for a moment, she was a deer kid again. Her large, oval ears quivered, listening, as deer do. Always listening, always hesitant, in case of danger.

She could sense, then hear some snuffling and scrunching sounds coming from the undergrowth. Suddenly Barton the Badger appeared from under a bush, waddling without looking, with his black and white striped face almost touching the ground.

He looked up, a little dazed, with soil particles clinging to his nose. He sneezed, and Dakota got a fright.

"Oh sorry Dakota," he said in his deep, badger voice. He scratched his silver tummy with his long claws.

"Anyhow, what are you going to do today?"

"Hello Barton," she replied, "Well….I was rather thinking of popping down to the farm lake for a drink of that lovely, clear water, in a minute." Her voice was silvery and smooth, almost like the sparkling, babbling water she was thinking about.

"Don't go there!" said Barton, rather hurriedly, looking a little scared. His ears flicked back and forth.

"Why ever not?" she asked.

"Because something's happening on the farm", he said. "There's lots of noise and humans and machines - it's best you stay away!"

With that, he scurried off quickly, his short legs working extra hard, and before she could ask him anything else.

Dakota was a little confused, and slightly afraid. She, like the other animals, had been vaguely aware of some rumbling and shaking, which, now that she thought about it, had woken her up. And if Barton felt nervous, then there was something to be nervous about.

She delicately picked her way through the forest, and hesitantly peeped out through the gently waving leaves at the group of farm buildings in the distance. A drop of rainwater fell on her face and ran down the side of her nose, just like a tear.

She sniffed the air for information. She could smell humans – different humans to the usual farm humans, and more than usual. She could also hear their voices, some sharp, some deep, floating to her in broken pieces on the breeze.

She was thirsty, and although she could easily lick the rain drops on the leaves to quench her thirst, she felt like taking a walk. She wondered if she should risk leaving the safety of the forest to walk down to the lake for a drink. She looked around for the other deer, seeking reassurance from the group. Some of them were rising or eating a little further away, so perhaps they hadn't yet heard the humans, and none of them seemed too worried yet.

If they weren't jittery, it was because most of the forest animals knew that some humans and their noisy machines lived at the farm, and the animals had learnt where to hide from them. Although it was very frightening and noisy, they had got somewhat use to the machines that caused a rumpus and threw up clouds of dust and plant particles in the fields at the end of summer and in autumn, for the harvest, and those that savagely pulled up and mutilated the ground in the winter and spring, to plant more crops.

But these didn't seem to be those machines or humans. Should she go for her drink?

While she was still watching, trying to decide, some movement at the lake's edge caught her eye. Lots of ducks and grebes and other birds regularly swam and nested there. But this was a brown furry flash in the sunlight, unlike feathers.

Suddenly a small creature darted across the field between the lake and the forest, running fast, smoothly and almost silently, like a river. The creature was coming straight towards Dakota! She jumped nimbly out of the way as it entered the forest and skidded to a halt; its black, shiny eyes looked surprised to see her there.

"My apologies if I frightened you", he said, talking slowly like a wise, old animal who considers every word.

Dakota looked at him, not quite sure what to make of his small, long body with smooth fur, his white chest and small rounded ears.

"I am Whanganui," he said. "I am a weasel."

He sounded serious and respectful, and although Dakota didn't really know what a weasel was, she bowed her head slightly and said politely: "Lovely to meet you sir. My name is Dakota, and I am a deer."

~~~~~~~~
~~~~~~~~

~ Chapter 2:
Whanganui's Past ~

All of a sudden a soft, thudding noise far away caught their attention. Whanganui and Dakota both looked apprehensively through the trees at the farm buildings, but they couldn't see anything specific. There were still some human voices and machine noises wafting over every now and then.

Dakota thought Whanganui seemed a little nervous and frightened, so she explained about the usual human activities and noises every change of season, which the resident animals were familiar with.

Whanganui nodded courteously, but seemed to know about this already. Then he cocked his head to one side, listening.

"But something else is afoot" Dakota said. "We don't know what, so we're a little worried, because it's not normal."

Whanganui nodded wisely, but didn't say anything yet.

The two of them decided to move into the safety of the middle of the forest, and Dakota took Whanganui to meet all the others.

She called all the deer, foxes, badgers, bats, hedgehogs, rabbits, squirrels, birds and other animals together. It took some time for everyone to arrive, because some animals were still sleeping, while others had wandered off to the edges of the forest, or into the fields alongside. The sleepy ones grumbled at being woken up and called so early, and the youngsters busy with their playful morning games had to be interrupted.

Once they were all gathered in the clearing, they stood or lay about in little groups. Some discussed the weather and the early rain and if they thought more rain was coming. Others moaned about the morning noises, complaining how they had been woken up, and questioning each other as to whether they thought the extra activity was anything other than the usual human interferences.

Dakota cleared her throat, and when she had everyone's attention, she explained about Whanganui. Most of the animals greeted and welcomed the newcomer enthusiastically. There were always those, however, who harboured some suspicion, and who grumbled at the back about new animals arriving and moving into their forest, who they felt didn't belong there.

It was clear that Whanganui wanted to say something, so the animals settled down to listen to his story.

He told them how he had come to be here, with them, in this forest. He said he had travelled far away from his home, leaving behind his friends and other weasels. He paused, looking sadly at the ground for a moment.

The animals looked around at each other, curious as to why anyone would want to leave their home. After all, it was not the way animals usually did things: you were born in a forest and lived and died there, and that was how it worked for most of them. Of course it was nature's way that some of the young, when they grew up, especially the male animals, would sometimes leave to search for new forests to live in, and wives to create families with, but the great majority of the animals in this forest had been here all their lives.

Whanganui described a time before his travels, when, just like this forest, he and some other animals had lived together in a forest near to some farm buildings. He described how his spouse had brought up seven weasel kits there. And like on this farm, Whanganui and his animal friends knew about the humans that lived there, and what sort of noises and disruptions to expect from them every now and then.

He continued, and explained what had happened to cause him and the others to leave so suddenly and unexpectedly.

He spoke of some terrible things that had happened, which had broken the peace there.

The animals listened in silence, with fear and panic mounting.

He described how one day many more humans and noisy machines had arrived.

The listening animals flicked their ears and looked around at each other nervously. Was this perhaps what was happening right at this moment, on their farm too?

Whanganui said the humans had walked into the forest, talking loudly and scaring the animals. They had made a lot of banging noises, putting up barriers. Then after many hours the humans had gone away.

He described how these obstacles had frightened and confused the animals, and how this meant some animals had to walk different ways to their usual paths to find food and get into their shelters.

Bentley the Bat, who was curled upside-down in a tree near to Whanganui, and who had a strong sense of injustice, squeaked "That's not right! Who do these humans think they are?"

Whanganui looked at him pensively, with unblinking eyes. He took a breath, as if about to say something, but stopped. He was sorry because he knew he had no answer for that important question.

Moxat the Muntjac Deer, who was half hidden under a bush, which was where he felt most comfortable, suddenly stepped forward, shaking some rain off his antlers. Because Moxat was small, many of the others didn't even notice him, and sometimes he took so long to work up enough courage to speak (being little and shy), that the other animals lost interest in what he had to say.

But Whanganui looked directly at him, and waited patiently for Moxat to speak.

"Erm," said Moxat, trying to clear his throat. His little voice never really carried far. His ears and small curved antlers twitched.

"I s-s-say w-w-we… must not trust the humans. W-w-we have heard and seen how they have taken t-t-trees and f-f-fields away from us…"

His voice trailed off. He had said more than he usually did, especially to a crowd, and he simply couldn't speak anymore. He bowed his head, and the others could briefly see his distinctive black V-mark etched between his eyes and perfectly curved, small horns. Then he carefully reversed back under the bush where he had been hiding.

Some unkind animals at the back sniggered, but Whanganui nodded respectfully in his direction, acknowledging what the Muntjac had said.

Then Whanganui continued his story.

He said although these disruptive actions by the humans on his farm had caused him and his animal friends great inconvenience, it had still been bearable compared to what had happened next.

The animals waited with bated breaths.

Whanganui went on. He told of how one day soon after that, the "terrible thing" had happened in his forest. He spoke of how this had caused all the animals in his forest to leave in a great hurry and become separated or lost He sorrowfully described how he didn't know where his spouse and kits were anymore.

Whanganui paused, because he knew what he was saying would terrify all the animals in his presence.

And when he did tell them all the details, it froze their hearts.

No one talked for a while. They had questions but they were too afraid to ask them.

Some of them wondered if all the new activity on their farm was something like that which Whanganui and his animal friends had experienced.

They all went off in little groups to contemplate and whisper about Whanganui's story.

Most were very worried about what he had described. They felt if it had happened once, in a very similar forest to theirs, then it might easily happen to them. Others weren't sure if they could fully believe what Whanganui had said — after all, the things he was claiming were unheard of, weren't they? And who was to say that

Whanganui was telling the truth? He had only just appeared and they didn't even know him!

But nevertheless, no matter what they thought or believed, everyone really hoped that a "terrible thing" would not happen to their forest too.

~~~~~~~~
~~~~~~~~

~ Chapter 3: The Meeting ~

A few days passed. The animal babies in the group were growing stronger and sometimes starting to come out of their dens and setts to play.

Barton and Balcombe and the other badgers proudly showed off their new badger cubs, who were now a few weeks older and just beginning to occasionally leave the sett and forage for themselves. When they did, often the adult and baby badgers happily played and jumped over tree stumps and each other.

Flint and some other foxes also had beautiful troops of pups, who were getting braver day by day; they gained speed and precision skills by running and falling over each other in play.

It was fun to watch their youthful playfulness, and Dakota, Whanganui and some of the other adult animals sometimes stood and watched the babies playing and rolling about, with joy in their hearts.

The animals hadn't forgotten what Whanganui had told them, but some whispered amongst themselves that he had only been trying to scare them, and that a "terrible thing" couldn't happen here, to them.

Some didn't want to imagine what it would be like if they all had to disperse and might not see each other again, like Whanganui and his animal friends. They talked in small groups about how something like Whanganui's experience couldn't really be possible, and how it would never happen. But they were all scared and no one knew what to do.

Eventually Tezcat the Tawny Owl, who was a natural leader on matters affecting everyone, decided to have a meeting. So he called together all the badgers, foxes, Whanganui the Weasel, the hedgehogs, squirrels, deer, bats, birds and rabbits.

Once they were all awake and had got the message, they congregated in an opening in the middle of the forest, where meetings were usually held. This always took quite a while, because some animals were a little lazier than others and took their time, and now that there were babies in many households too, it took time to get them there.

Tezcat yawned, as he wasn't used to being awake during the day, but this was important. He sidled a little along his favourite branch, which was in the perfect place, not too high and not too low. He could view the animals below and around him, and they could see and hear him speak.

His large, dark eyes blinked a few times as he surveyed the pairs and groups of animals standing or lying down attentively before him, or in nearby trees. Whanganui was leaning on a tree root just below him, with his bright and watchful eyes focused on Tezcat.

"Dear animals," Tezcat said, "I have called you here today, because there is an important matter that needs to be discussed."

He flapped his wings for a moment to stretch them, and the dark brown and white striped pattern of his wing feathers caught a ray of sunshine. Most of the animals waited quietly for him to speak, but there was a little rustling and mumbling to the side, where a hedgehog and rabbit seemed to be in some sort of disagreement, but they stopped as soon as the other animals looked their way.

"Whanganui the Weasel," Tezcat stated, "has told us something of grave concern."

Some of the animals nodded, grunted or whined in agreement. Others muttered, but it wasn't possible to tell if they agreed or not.

Tezcat looked intensely at them all with wisdom in his eyes and continued: "We have seen some extra activity in the past few days. We have seen more humans, and they have been making more noise than before."

"We need a strategy," he announced.

There was some murmuring and shuffling amongst the animals at the back. Finally some of the deer and rabbits stepped forward.

"We don't believe anything bad is going to happen," one of the deer complained.

This made the others who wanted to argue feel braver. A rabbit hopped into the open.

"Just because there's a little bit of extra noise from the humans, doesn't mean anything like Whanganui says is going to happen. I think he exaggerated it anyway!" she exclaimed, then looked around for some support from her group. She didn't want to look directly at Whanganui. One or two other rabbits nodded vehemently, while others looked away.

"Yes…" agreed one of the squirrels, climbing down from his tree branch and stiffly waving his fluffy tail in an agitated way, "…there's really not enough evidence!"

Moxat the Muntjac, who as you know was much smaller than the other deer and consequently quite timid, tried to speak.

"A-a-a-and…and…" He trailed off because he was so frightened of talking to a large group, and some of the animals at the back mumbled rudely and weren't prepared to listen.

"Let Moxat have his say", said Tezcat authoritatively. Tezcat fixed his shiny eyes intensely on the dissident animals, and they quickly became quiet.

Moxat tried again: "W-w-w-well, it's just that things h-h-haven't always st-st-stayed the same in this forest." He swallowed, then continued:

"Our a-a-ancestors lived different l-l-lives. Sh-sh-surely this means we c-c-cannot trust that things will c-c-continue as they always have?"

His little voice faltered.

The animals grunted or barked, some in agreement and some not. They looked at Tezcat and Whanganui for confirmation.

Tezcat sighed deeply and ruffled his feathers, while Whanganui didn't say anything but nodded his head dolefully.

With that, the animals all turned to their neighbours and started arguing loudly with each other. Those who thought the humans were about to do something bad were trying to shout above those who insisted that nothing would happen and life would continue as normal.

As you can imagine, no one was really listening to anyone else. In fact, their arguing drowned out the noises of some more human and machine activities down on the farm.

Eventually Tezcat waved one of his taloned feet to quieten everyone. It took a while for them to calm down, and when they were all paying attention again, he said:

"My animal friends, we cannot beat around the bush, as we say. Something different is happening. This is not in question anymore. We can all see with our own eyes and hear with our own ears that the humans at the farm buildings are planning something.

"We cannot ignore the fact that something has changed. And if we do nothing, and then something like Whanganui has predicted does happen, what then?"

Those who didn't agree were now silent, because they respected Tezcat, and they had to admit, he did have a point. They looked around at each other, then quietened down.

Tezcat called Flint the Fox to the front. She walked quickly and gracefully, her padded feet making almost no sound as she stepped forward. Her bright, brown eyes looked questioningly at Tezcat, and her ears stood up, listening attentively.

"Flint, you are quick and silent. When you go at night to the farm buildings, you are to look out for anything unusual or out of place, and report this back to us."

Flint bowed her head slightly and twitched her beautiful, fuzzy tail. She was proud to be chosen for this special role, and happily accepted.

Tezcat then asked Rima the Rabbit to step up. She hopped to the mossy place beneath Tezcat's tree, then stood up on her hind legs, so she could see better, and her long, soft ears shivered in anticipation.

"Rima, you are fast and small. This makes you perfect for the role of our messenger – if we need to tell the animals about anything urgent or important, you are to let all the animals know as quickly as you can."

Rima beamed because Tezcat had chosen her, out of all the rabbits and other animals, to do something as important as this.

Finally Tezcat asked Bentley the Bat to be part of the "strategy team", as he called it. Bentley was only just awake, because like Tezcat, he was usually a nocturnal animal. He blinked, and sniffed his little shrivelled nose as he waited for Tezcat to speak.

"Bentley, you can fly swiftly and unseen, so you are to do some aerial investigations at night, and let us know if you see anything different or concerning."

Bentley, like Flint and Rima, was pleased and honoured to have been chosen by Tezcat, when there were so many worthy animals. Besides a little grunting in the bushes from a hedgehog and a rabbit, who seemed to be arguing about the suitability of the chosen animals, it seemed that all the animals approved.

It was then agreed that the five animals in the "strategy team" (that is Flint, Rima, Bentley, Whanganui and Tezcat) would meet every night after any investigations, and decide on any further actions if the need arose.

The other animals, now satisfied that something was being done, all wandered off to either eat or sleep, depending on what their species normally did at that time of the day.

~~~~~~~~~
~~~~~~~~~

~ Chapter 4: The Serpent Arrives ~

A few days later, Dakota was enjoying munching some ivy leaves in the sunshine which filtered through the trees. Occasionally she was lucky enough to find some leaves with a drop or two of dew on them which hadn't yet dried up. She eyed the sky through the leaves, searching for rain clouds, but for now, the clouds were only wisps.

Dakota and her herd of deer were quite near the edge of the forest, but as it was near midday, most didn't feel brave enough to step completely out of the forest. Many were relaxing, happily lying around in shaded and cool parts of the forest and chewing their cud, as they tended to do in the daylight hours.

Dakota stopped for a moment to admire the different colours and shapes of the leaves, now all beautiful shades of green. Some were a light mint green, others were a deeper emerald green, while the older leaves had yellow or white patches and patterns drizzled over them, which seemed to zig zag and wave as they twirled and fluttered in the light breeze.

Next thing, Dakota noticed some movement out of the corner of her eye. She turned for a closer look, and in the distance she could just make out a group of humans starting to walk up the muddy track which lead from the farm buildings to the forest.

Tezcat the Tawny Owl was sitting in a nearby tree, and he yawned, annoyed at being woken up at this time.

"Dakota, what are you staring at?" he asked in a tired drawl, ruffling his feathers in a flustered way.

"Oh, Tezcat, I think the humans are ….." but she couldn't finish her sentence, because she felt a wave of panic rising in her throat.

Just at that moment, Rima the Rabbit came sprint-hopping into the forest, completely out of breath, and braked, throwing up dirt and leaves.

"Tezcat and Dakota, oh dear… I think it's today! They're coming..." and with that, she sped off to warn more animals.

In the next few minutes, there was lots of panicked activity and discussion among the animals, but no one could agree on what to do. Some ran around in circles, unsure whether to run away or stay and hide. Others froze on the spot, not sure if there was any point in running at this stage, or where they would run to.

During the past few nights, Flint the Fox and Bentley the Bat had been doing their 'special investigations' at the farm buildings, but hadn't reported anything to warrant more concern.

The foxes and badgers and other burrowing animals ran into their earthy homes and hid away with their young, as deep into their holes as they could go. After all, it was doubtful that the very young animals would be able to keep up if their parents ran too far.

Many of the deer started fleeing hastily across the fields, away from the oncoming mass of humans and machines. Luckily most of the kids, with their long and spindly legs, were able to run fast. Some remaining animals looked around for hiding places in the forest, confused and worried.

Meanwhile Dakota, Tezcat, and some of the other deer and animals stayed for now, peeping out of the foliage and trying to work out exactly what the humans were doing.

The animals soon had to move deeper into the forest, as the group of humans with some small machines got closer and closer. The animals could smell them and hear their jarring voices and raucous laughter.

Eventually the humans arrived, and set themselves up with lots of talking, shouting, banging and clattering. (It sounded to the animals almost like their own busy discussions from a few days ago, only much noisier). Then the humans moved through the outer edge of the forest, and started cutting away and pulling up some small bushes and trees, hammering in poles, and generally battering, pounding and stomping around.

By now, most of the animals had left, running out of the forest. A few had remained in the forest, quivering with fear in their underground burrows, in the undergrowth, or up in the trees if they were lucky or skilled enough to get there.

To those animals who were able to observe what the humans were doing (such as the birds and squirrels in the trees above), it seemed very destructive. Some of them shuddered to see what the humans were doing, and shrank fearfully into the corners of the branches or under the leaves high up, trying not to be seen.

It took many hours. In all that time, the animals who were hiding pressed themselves deep into their hiding places, and didn't eat or really sleep either. They were too scared.

The noise and carnage in the forest continued.

Eventually, after what seemed like all day, the humans started packing up, all the while shouting and laughing and waving their arms and occasionally dropping tools with caused sharp metallic clangs. Then they grouped together and finally walked away with their tools, back towards the farm buildings.

Once it was quiet, and only then, did some of the bravest animals begin to come out of their shelters hesitantly, carefully sniffing the air. The smell of humans, their sweat, and the freshly butchered trees and plants were strong in their nostrils. They twitched their ears and noses apprehensively at these unfamiliar sights and smells.

Only then did the less brave animals and those further afield also begin to creep out of their retreats and hiding places and trickle back to the forest.

The animals looked around in amazement and horror at what they saw. Some of their walking and feeding pathways were now barricaded off, and their favourite bushes chopped away. Branches had been torn off some of the trees and were lying on the ground, where they had been tossed carelessly and thoughtlessly. The humans seemed to have dropped some small items in the forest too – some of these objects smelt of food, whilst others twirled and flittered every time there was a little breeze, or got caught in branches where they flailed hopelessly to get free.

The animals felt that their forest had been invaded and violated.

But the most awful and surprising thing was a strange, bright orange and smooth, snake-like creature, which formed a huge, caged-in area.

It stood taller than any deer but was thinner than most insects. It twisted and flapped and writhed its plastic way around a roughly rectangular shape which started inside some of the edge of the forest, the part nearest to the farm buildings, and then continued out of the forest and around the field. The lake where the animals liked to drink was trapped inside this barrier.

Wooden and metal poles had been banged into the ground at regular intervals, which constrained the pliable orange creature, so it couldn't break free in the wind, as it seemed to want to do.

It looked like an enormous orange serpent, which rattled and shook in the breeze as if it were alive. The animals shrank in fear from it.

As if that weren't enough, just then there was a commotion from the inside of this terrible creature. The animals could hear some ducklings quacking and crying out for their mother, who was outside the barrier, running alongside it in panic.

Dakota called to the mother duck. "What's wrong?"

"My babies, oh my babies!" mum cried back. "They're inside this thing and I can't get them out!"

Whanganui, who had a long, flexible body and short legs close to the ground, seemed to know what to do. He rushed up to where the distressed ducklings were, and contorted and wriggled his way under the orange serpent. Then he pushed his back up against the orange material, which luckily yielded a little to this force, and the ducklings were able to run out of the small space he had made, back to their mother. "Oh, thank you, thank you," she sobbed.

The other animals nearby watched in admiration and relief.

However the signs of the devastation from the humans were still all around them. The animals looked at each other, hoping for answers that no one seemed to be able to give.

"What does it mean?" asked Barton, eyeing the orange serpent with distrust. His ears were flat against his head.

Tezcat and Whanganui looked anxiously at each other, then turned slowly to face the other animals.

"It has started," said Whanganui sadly. He looked frazzled and beaten, as if he had fought and lost many battles.

"The humans are here. It is coming soon," he said in a frail and faint voice.

~~~~~~~~
~~~~~~~~

KATHRYN ROSE NEWEY

~ Chapter 5: Decisions To Make ~

It was clear now to most of the animals that their world was changing. The humans were up to something, and the animals weren't sure yet what it was, but they knew they didn't like it.

Tezcat called another meeting, because they needed to decide what to do about this latest development. In actual fact, Tezcat was a little unsure about what to do, which was unusual for him, so he thought a gathering might generate some discussion and suggestions from the animals.

Once all the animals had grouped again beneath Tezcat's tree, he looked carefully at them all. Being a leader, he felt part of his job was to be strong, wise and direct, so that the other animals felt secure. He didn't want to admit to the others that he wasn't sure this time how to respond to what the humans had done, because he knew the other animals might feel more scared if he was confused.

So Tezcat pulled himself up to his full height (which wasn't very large, but luckily he had the added height of the tree) and fluffed out his feathers, then cleared his throat.

"My friends…" he began.

"We cannot lose hope. We cannot stand by and let these bad things happen to us.…"

He paused.

"Yes," squeaked Bentley the Bat, hanging upside down from a nearby branch. "We must do something to stop these humans!" His small, dark and wrinkled face and delicate ears trembled with tension and excitement.

The animals started murmuring and talking in small groups. They all had some opinion on the recent events, and almost all spoke at once, so that no one was really listening to what his neighbour had to say.

Eventually Barton, Balcombe and Flint stepped forward with a suggestion. Once everyone was quiet and were willing to pay attention again, they spoke.

"I think we need to tear down the orange serpent", said Flint. Some animals looked shocked at her suggestion. After all, they didn't know Flint as being quite as radical as this.

"Yes," agreed Balcombe. "If we take away what shouldn't be here in the first place, then it wouldn't be wrong."

The animals all turned to their neighbours to discuss whether an action like this would be the right or wrong thing to do, or whether it mattered, because after all, it was the animals' forest, wasn't it? Not everyone agreed on what the best way forward was, and the discussions got quite rowdy.

Rima hopped forward. Although she was small, somehow her presence commanded calm and respect. Everyone quietened down and waited for her to speak. Her long, rounded ears stood straight and tall.

"Taking down the orange serpent sounds like a good idea," she said, "but how on earth are we going to remove it? Most of us are simply not big or strong enough!"

Many of the animals nodded quietly at Rima's logical statement; they could see what she said made sense. Of course, some animals were still afraid of the serpent. They thought it was a living creature and most certainly too dangerous to tamper with. Yet again, this created another animated discussion amongst everyone. So once again the forest was alive with the whining, grunting, chirping and barking of all the animals talking at once.

Some of the animals felt that taking away what the humans had put there wouldn't make any difference, because the humans would simply come back and do it all again.

Others argued that removing the serpent would send a strong message to the humans that they and their machines and orange serpents were not welcome in the animals' forest.

Still others (but only a few) at the back argued in hushed tones amongst themselves that they couldn't possibly take the serpent away, as it would most certainly retaliate and hurt or even kill them.

Eventually one of the deer stepped forward. He was a tall and strong buck, with a proud pair of antlers.

"I have a better idea", he announced.

"What if we all lined up and refused to move next time the humans come… what if we simply stood firm and didn't let them into our forest?" he asked, puffed up with his unique idea.

Someone laughed nervously at the back, then looked around in dismay when no one else laughed.

One of the squirrels shimmied down the tree to where he could see everyone.

"That's the most ridiculous thing I've ever heard," he shouted in his tiny voice. "It's alright for you deer – you're the largest animals, but how are the rest of us small animals going to make any difference?"

He sounded quite cross, and jerked his tail irritably.

Some of the animals at the back hadn't heard him because even when he shouted, his voice wasn't particularly loud. So there was a mumbling from those who hadn't heard, and then more mumbling from those who had heard it, repeating it for the benefit of the ones at the back.

Then once again, everyone turned to the animals next to them and started arguing.

The combined noise of all the animals bickering drowned out the sounds of more banging, drilling and clanging which had started up and was coming from the other side of the forest.

One or two animals at the edge of the group thought they heard something, and stopped in the middle of their quarrel to cock their heads to one side and listen. But the cacophony of animal noises was so loud and discordant that those few animals who thought they heard something concluded it must have been just more animals squabbling, or perhaps only the wind.

Eventually Tezcat stopped them.

"My dear friends," he said.

"This thing affects us all. We need to be united in our actions. We cannot fight with one another. Who will be left to defend us against what the humans are doing?"

Most of the animals felt guilty and silly now. They looked sheepishly at their neighbours who they had been shouting at moments ago. Many realised they needed to work together on this thing - this possible "terrible thing" the humans were bringing to the forest.

Unfortunately there were still those animals who bore a grudge. One of the hedgehogs now refused to talk to his neighbour, a rabbit, because they had disagreed so vehemently about what they each thought the humans were doing.

The rabbit, who was generally more mobile than the hedgehog, insisted that there were many more humans than animals – he said he had seen them with his own eyes! The hedgehog sniffed in disdain and begged to differ. He had only seen the humans from afar, and through his blurry eyes which weren't much good these days at seeing anything further than his nose (neither of which he would admit to), but he said it couldn't possibly be so – he retaliated that there were only a handful of humans who could be easily overcome by the animals, and he should know, because he said he had checked on them every day!

Finally, Whanganui stepped up to talk. Everyone quietened down to give the newcomer a chance.

"Friends," he said, "we must decide here and now to do something, something the humans would not expect from us. But I warn you, the humans will not be easily stopped. I know this from my time before."

The animals were confused now – it seemed that Whanganui was saying the destruction by the humans was inevitable and there was nothing they could really do which would make a significant difference.

But Whanganui continued.

"We should do everything you have suggested today." The animals looked perplexed at this.

He went on: "The larger animals must stand firm in a line to stop the humans next time they come.

"In the meantime, everyone should try to break down some of the orange serpent. Even if you bite or tear a small part, it will still be an important contribution."

Even those who didn't agree before thought this sounded like something they could all be part of. There were still some arguments, but they were a little less noisy than before. Even the argumentative rabbit and hedgehog grumbled in tentative agreement with each other.

The animals started to move off and get on with their day.

Some of them were even determined to go immediately to the orange serpent, and start biting and clawing it to pieces, and indeed they did.

~~~~~~~~
~~~~~~~~

74

~ Chapter 6: Someone Goes Missing ~

For the next few days, most of the animals stayed in the forest or close to its perimeter. Everyone was nervous, wondering what dreadful fate might befall them. However, some of the braver ones had ventured out to the orange serpent, mostly at night, and had started chewing or ripping at it. In some places, it was beginning to look a little tattered, but you had to be close up to actually see the damage.

Some of the animals still refused to believe fully that anything worse could or would come to their forest. They often stood chattering in little groups, discussing the day the humans had come, and trying to fathom what the orange serpent was there for, and whether it was dangerous. They hadn't yet been brave enough to go right up to it, even though Whanganui assured them it wasn't alive.

Nevertheless, they complained how their forest had been disturbed and plundered, and they moaned that they now had to find alternative transport routes, different plants for feeding and other sources of water. They lamented about how their young couldn't get around or under the orange serpent, or were too afraid of it. They shook and shuddered and snivelled with the bad memory, fear and inconvenience of it all.

But unfortunately, and unbeknown to them, there was worse to come.

~~~~~~~~

One early morning soon after, when Dakota and some of the other deer were only just awake and had started grazing on some fresh grass and
~~~~~~~~

leaves, Barton and Balcombe the Badgers came loping into the deer's area, looking all around and clearly very upset.

"Have you seen Moxat?" Balcombe managed to blurt out, in between short breaths. She was obviously worried, as she couldn't stop pacing around and shaking, even as she spoke.

"No," said Dakota. "Where did you see him last?"

Balcombe and Barton both spoke at once. Dakota looked from one to the other, confused.

"Let me speak, dear," said Barton.

He explained that Moxat, being so shy, had felt reassured if he foraged at night near to the badgers. "We look out for him," explained Barton.

He described how, as usual, this had happened the night before. They had all moved around and fed in the forest and towards the edge of the forest.

Barton said they were almost sure that everyone, including Moxat, had come back in the early hours of the morning to the centre of the forest, where their homes or hiding places were, and had gone to sleep.

"But now that we think of it, what with all the baby badgers to keep an eye on, it's getting a little complicated to know where everyone is at all times," said Balcombe.

"It's possible we might not have noticed if he was with us when we returned". Barton hung his head in shame at this admission.

Balcombe added: "We've thought so hard about where he could be, but we're at a loss."

Then she wailed "Oh, poor Moxat, he'll be so scared if we've left him alone," and started pacing again.

Dakota suggested they get all the larger deer together and go searching.

"Don't you worry," she assured them, "we'll find him."

Most of the deer and some other animals, including Whanganui, Rima and some birds decided to join the search.

They spread out, walking, hopping or flying carefully through the trees, and calling the little Muntjac Deer's name. But they didn't find him there.

Eventually they grouped back together in the middle of the forest. Barton and Balcombe looked up hopefully as they arrived, but Dakota shook her head sadly.

Whanganui suggested the larger animals try looking further afield. It was now later in the morning, and not too hot, so some of the herd of deer agreed to leave the woods and look in the neighbouring fields of the farm.

Meticulously the deer walked and scanned the fields, first one field then another. They searched the field inside the orange serpent and outside it. It helped that some animals had bitten and torn holes in the serpent, so they were able to force through it or get around it in various places.

Again and again they called the little Muntjac's name, but to no avail. They were hot and thirsty now, so took a moment to drink the cool water from the farm lake, before making their way back through the orange serpent and into the forest where the others waited.

There was some consternation about them walking into the middle of the orange serpent. Some animals looked at them in disbelief, while others were worried the deer had somehow been contaminated or hurt.

But Whanganui pressed on: "There is only one other place to look.

"I do not like to speak of it, for it may bring great sadness."

The deer and other animals waited expectantly, with fear in their hearts.

"My friends," said Whanganui, "we must search the long strip behind the forest, where the humans' noisy, metal machines run fast and dangerously."

Some of the deer, who were more experienced at crossing the human roads, agreed to search there. They didn't want to tell everyone, but they knew this place could be one of injury and death. From time to time, they had seen an animal get hurt or be killed there by these impossibly quick and monstrous machines that bore down on the animal before it could get out of the way.

With heavy hearts, four of the deer moved through the forest, towards this awful and disturbing place.

Most of the animals kept their distance from this edge of the forest, if they could. The droning sounds of the hurtling, ferocious human machines were constant; the sounds travelled through the trees, sometimes loud and intrusive continually, sometimes growling and zooming and whooshing irregularly.

The thick trees at the side of the road acted like a sound barrier, so not all noise got through, but the animals were used to hearing it in the distance, almost all the time. It was of course quieter at night, because there were fewer cars, but in the silence of the night, even one car's rushing sounds whizzed and whipped through the forest into every animals' weary ears.

The searching deer walked slower and more hesitantly as they neared the edge of the forest alongside the road. When they got there, they waited, hidden in the woods, until they could hear the birdsong again. Then they knew no car monsters were coming, but they were aware that some may come again at any moment.

The deer walked hurriedly and nervously up and down the roadside closest to the woods, but they didn't see anything, and they were worried because they could hear some distant sounds of cars growing louder.

They were just about to give up their search, when one of the deer called out. He was standing near to a little bundle of fur on the roadside. The others rushed over, but they all had to pull back into the woods as an enormous, roaring truck surged down the road and shook the ground as it passed.

As soon as it was gone, the deer stepped out. There was Moxat the Muntjac, lying crumpled on his side, thrown carelessly onto the edge of the road. A pool of almost dry blood was on the ground below his mouth.

The larger deer clustered around him, tenderly turning him over and carefully nudging him with their hooves.

But he didn't move. It was too late. There was nothing they could do.

After a while, they trudged sorrowfully back to the middle of the forest, where everyone had gathered, and told them the bad news.

"But why?" sobbed Rima when she heard. "Why do these humans with their fast, metal machines kill us?"

Dakota pawed the ground mournfully and added: "What did Moxat ever do to them? He didn't deserve this!"

Tezcat flapped his wings, as if to call everyone's attention, but his wings made hardly any sound. In any case, most animals were there already, waiting quietly, as they had heard about Moxat's disappearance and had gathered worriedly in the forest clearing.

Tezcat cleared his throat and said some kind words about Moxat. He spoke of how, despite his timidity, Moxat had been loved. He proclaimed that Moxat would continue to be remembered with great fondness.

Some animals sobbed or whined softly when he said these words.

With great heartache and bewilderment, the animals then peeled off alone or in small clusters to quiet corners of the forest, to wonder and worry about Moxat's cruel and pointless fate.

~~~~~~~~~
~~~~~~~~~

88

~ Chapter 7: Forest Grove ~

It wasn't until early the next morning, at sunrise as they rose, that one of the four deer who had found Moxat's body suddenly remembered seeing something else at the side of the road, something unusual.

At the time, she had been so concerned about Moxat that she hadn't registered something different.

She discussed it with the other deer, and they agreed to go back to the strip of road to check.

Once they got there, and had patiently waited for a break between the motoring monsters, they could see two enormous rectangular shapes, each on two thick and sturdy poles, standing proudly up against the trees, facing the road in both directions.

When they were sure there were no cars, the deer stepped out and peered at them, trying to make sense of the many marks and images on the boards. There were pictures of some humans, two adults and two young, smiling broadly, in front of some buildings like the farm buildings the animals knew.

The animals couldn't read, unfortunately, but if they had been able to, this is what they would have seen:

Ten Luxury Homes Coming Soon!

Forest Grove – Beautiful Homes in Natural Surroundings.

Forest Pathways and Bicycle Trails.

Wildlife on your Doorstep.

Only 45 Minutes Commute to London.

Book your Viewing NOW – 0865 123 9999

Had they been able to read the words, then consternation, outrage and anger would have resulted. Had they been capable of understanding the words, they would have fretted about the pathways through their forest, and the buildings (which would be homes for humans), so close to their animal homes. And had they known how to decode human language, they wouldn't have liked to be described as "wildlife", especially not "on the doorstep" of the humans.

But as it was, none of the animals could read or decipher anything on those signs.

As they were trying to analyse these new eyesores, the deer averted their eyes from the lump that was Moxat's little body, still lying at the edge of the road, tiny and silent. They knew there was nothing more they could do for Moxat, and that the way of nature was for the crows and other scavengers to help to decompose and digest his small body over the next few weeks, until there was almost nothing there, perhaps just a little piece of fur where Moxat had once been.

They felt a burning anger that this was not a normal death, and that Moxat had been slaughtered by a careless human driver in his fast and brutal road machine, who had then left Moxat there to die. Other than that, they struggled to understand how and why this had happened; but they knew it was not the way of nature for animals to die like this.

When the deer got back inside the forest, they reported the huge and confusing sign boards to the others, but no one, including Tezcat or Whanganui, could really add any insight into what the boards were, or why they were there. Of course they realised that the boards were something the humans must have put there, considering there were humans pictured on them, but after a lot of discussion with all the animals (and some more arguing, especially between the hedgehog and the rabbit who were neighbours and who sorely disagreed on most things), they couldn't really decide on any particular action.

It was still early morning, so the animals moved off, some to graze and some to sleep.

Before they had finished chewing their first mouthful, or had had a chance to say "good morning" to their friends, Rima hastily thumped up to them and told them a group of humans was coming this way.

"But," she said, "it's a bit strange… they're young humans."

She sped off to let more animals know.

Despite the news that the humans were younger and smaller than usual, most of the animals panicked, thinking this was something to do with the "terrible thing" again – perhaps it was about to happen? Some animals decided to run away and hide themselves deep in the woods or in their holes. Some of the deer fled across the fields, forgetting how they had previously discussed that they would stand firm and refuse the humans entry to their forest.

Dakota and some others wanted to stay and observe, because smaller humans didn't seem as threatening as those from last time, and they were curious as to why the humans and their machines would send their young.

So the few animals who dared to, watched carefully through the foliage, as a group of perhaps only five young humans of varying sizes, made their way up the farm track towards the forest. When the humans were closer, the animals could see they were carrying rectangular boards – not as large as the ones on the roadside, but boards nevertheless with similar marks and symbols which the animals couldn't see clearly from a distance, but wouldn't have been able to understand even if they could see them.

Suddenly loud and reverberating noises of machinery started up at the farm, and lots of human voices (this time from the older humans) cut through the breeze like growls. This seemed to have an effect on the young humans, who started in fright, then jabbered away quickly and excitedly to each other. They slowed their walk and turned to face the farm buildings and human activity there. Then they stopped and appeared to form a loosely structured line across the road.

Dakota whispered to the other animals: "Look, they're lining up across the road, standing firm, just like our buck said we should!" The animals were incredulous – it did indeed seem that the young humans were creating a barrier with their bodies.

The larger group of humans and their monstrous machines started their rattling and roaring advance up the slight slope of the farm track towards the forest, and towards the young humans.

The young humans stood steadfast.

Eventually, after what seemed like an eternity, the older humans and machines had almost reached the young humans, and they stopped, shuddering to an uneasy and temporary halt. Two older humans marched angrily up to the younger ones.

"Just what do you think you're doing?" shouted one of the older humans. He glared at the children.

Of course, to the watching animals, they only heard and saw angry gestures and quick, harsh sounds, because they couldn't understand the words of human language. But they knew enough to realise that the older humans didn't like what the younger humans were doing, and the animals found themselves feeling sorry for, and protective of the young humans.

"W-w-we don't think you should do this…" stammered one of the young humans.

"There are animals in the forest, and we're here to protect them!" declared another bravely.

"What twaddle!" roared one of the men.

"You're trespassing, and you've got exactly two minutes to get out of the way, or I'll call the police!"

The animals watched with trepidation. Had they known what the young humans were attempting, they might have rushed out and joined their protest. But all they could do was watch and wait silently and nervously, ready to flee if necessary.

The conversation between the older and younger humans continued for a few minutes, and although still fraught, it became clear the younger ones had said something to convince the older ones. Suddenly the older humans turned around and signalled to their troops to back off and go home.

"It's not happening today, men," shouted one of them. Because he was facing away, the young humans and animals didn't see how he winked as he made his announcement to the other humans near to him.

The younger humans cheered and 'high-fived' each other's hands in glee, elated with their victory. The animals watched as the younger humans eventually disappeared down the track, after the groups of older humans and noisy machines had made their way back to the farmyard.

A few moments later, all that was left was some dust where they had been, and some soft thudding and knocking sounds coming from the farmyard as the humans packed away and then left for the day.

The animals looked at each other cautiously, not quite believing what they had just witnessed. Then they moved off to tell the others the good news.

The contrary rabbit and hedgehog, though, weren't as easily appeased. The rabbit insisted that the young humans must have bared their teeth and claws – how else would they have turned away the larger and stronger humans? But, as the young humans didn't have large teeth or claws, he was sure the older humans would simply be back at another time.

The hedgehog, on the other hand, whose primary method of defence was rolling into a ball with his spikes turned outward, insisted that the young humans had used their boards like spikes to try to impale the older humans with. He knew, he said with authority, that the older humans had got the message and wouldn't ever come back because he claimed spikes were always an effective defence mechanism.

At this point the rabbit and hedgehog both harrumphed, turned their backs on each other, and stomped away in opposite directions.

~~~~~~~~
~~~~~~~~

~ Chapter 8: More Trouble ~

The rest of the animals couldn't quite grasp their good fortune.

The young humans had seemed to have an amazing effect on the older humans and their raucous machines. The animals wondered what the young humans had communicated that had caused such a definite about-turn in the intentions of the older humans and their machinery.

But they didn't need to wonder or celebrate for too long, because unfortunately for them, it didn't last.

~~~~~~~~
~~~~~~~~

Around two days afterwards, Flint and Bentley had returned from their nocturnal investigations and reported some extra goings-on at the farm buildings. In fact they couldn't be quite sure, but it seemed as if there was a new monster machine inhabiting the farmyard.

When questioned a little more closely by Tezcat and Whanganui, they said the new machine had a tall sheltered space up high for a human to sit inside, which was mostly transparent. They reported that the contraption seemed to have only two feet, but they were wide and oval and heavy-looking, and stretched all the way under each side of its belly.

However the most frightening part of the machine, they claimed (and their voices became quieter as they described this), was its mouth, which was enormous and open all the time, and had huge jagged teeth along the bottom edge.

Bentley added that the mouth and teeth were so heavy, that the monster had to rest it on the ground. Then Flint unhelpfully suggested that the mouth was big enough to scoop up a number of animals in its jaws at once. Everyone shivered when she said this.

Actually most of the animals had heard and felt some clangourous and reverberant activity over the past few days, during the daytime, while many of them were resting or sleeping. Some had peered through the trees and had seen and heard humans and their monster machines moving about.

But by now they had started to accept the fact that the humans seemed determined to undertake something momentous and probably destructive. Some of the more wary and cynical animals were now beginning to see that

Whanganui may have been right about some of the things he'd warned them about, after all.

Even the ill-natured hedgehog and obnoxious rabbit more or less agreed, for once, that something bad was afoot, and that they needed to be on high alert. The hedgehog then suggested that perhaps it might be a good idea for them to warn each other, should anything terrible happen, and the rabbit grudgingly consented to this arrangement.

~~~~~~~~

On the morning of the third day, the animals awoke to hard, driving rain. It was the kind of rain which is relentless, which runs down your ears and legs and gets into your eyes, which soaks your fur and makes you feel miserable and cold, no matter where you hide.
~~~~~~~~

The rain falling against the orange serpent caused a dull pattern of beats which was never ending; the animals tossed and turned in their burrows and pressed their ears close to their heads to try to escape the rhythmic thuds, but it was impossible. And when the wind blew, pieces of the orange serpent ripped and slapped loudly against the poles, as if it was trying to tear itself away from that place.

Through the dense rain, there were suddenly some deep, rumbling and thunderous sounds which slunk through the ground and convulsed into the animals' bodies.

Dakota shuddered. Before she had properly opened her eyes, she could smell, then hear the humans. More than usual. Their voices rose and fell indistinctly through the pelting rain; the rain couldn't quite drown them out, even though it seemed to try.

The deer and some other animals snuck warily to the edge of the forest and peeped out towards the farm. The rumbling vibrations seemed to be coming from a large machine, with a huge mouth at its front – this must be the monster which Flint and Bentley had reported! Lots of humans were milling around, some standing and talking, some collecting up tools and machines. Despite the heavy rain, clattering and clanging sounds reached the animals' wet ears, and they flicked them, almost as if they hoped they could fling away the discordant sounds and the humans that made them.

Then the colossal scoop-machine roared loudly and started rolling slowly but determinedly towards the forest. Now the vibrations seemed to rock everything, including the animals' hearts against the ribs in their chests.

Dakota let out a series of short barks, to alert the other deer and animals to danger. All the animals started rushing out of their burrows, dens and nests – Flint the fox and her cubs, Barton, Balcombe and the other badgers and cubs, Bentley and the other bats, the other deer, the rabbits and squirrels, the hedgehogs and the birds. They were joined by Whanganui who came running up from the lake, as well as some ducks.

It all happened so fast that poor Rima, who was supposed to be the emergency messenger, was only just out of her burrow, and didn't have time to warn everyone. She darted around as best she could, trying desperately to find everyone and to wake those who might still be asleep, but the anxious noises of the other animals had alerted most by now anyway.

As you can imagine, the animals made alarmed, rowdy and confused noises, because so many were crying out as they ran or flew. It sounded like lots of different birds learning to sing and not getting the notes on time. This wasn't helped by the pouring rain, which dulled and distorted their warning calls, and made everything wet and muddy, so some animals slipped and fell as they stampeded in panic and fear.

The humans and their tools and machines, including the newest and largest monster-mouth machine, were walking and rumbling in a purposeful way up the farm track towards the forest. The unyielding rain and the resultant slippery mud everywhere may have slowed them slightly, making manoeuvring difficult, but it didn't seem to deter their intentions, and they kept coming.

Tezcat, Whanganui and Dakota were trying to calm the animals, but their appeals were lost in the racket and chaos. Eventually some of the animals, especially the deer and larger mammals, ran away across the fields. They streamed off in different directions, not sure where they were headed or who to follow.

"Where will you go in this rain?" shouted Dakota after them, but her words were whipped away and no one answered her.

The humans and their machinery had reached the bottom edge of the orange serpent, and they aggressively hacked and slashed some of it away, without needing much effort.

Then, with much roaring and lurching, the monster-mouth machine and its human navigator entered the field and started advancing slowly and menacingly along the edge of the orange serpent. The monster's huge mouth scraped along and into the ground, forcing up enormous chunks of soil, rocks and bushes as it went.

The remaining animals watched in fear as the monster kept ploughing and mowing up everything in its path. The whining and screaming and pulsating noises it made were terrifying. It moved along all the way across the bottom edge of the orange serpent, then wobbled and screeched around and began moving along the next row, tearing up and destroying all life in its path.

The rain kept falling, as if trying to make it difficult for the machine and its human, but they didn't stop. The machine was too large and too forceful; nothing could halt its wreckage.

As if this weren't frightening enough, two more humongous machines droned and howled onto the field. One had an almighty arm with a large mouth at the end (not quite as big as the mouth of the monster-mouth, but still formidable), which it used for heaving up rockloads of trees and branches and mud from the growing pile created as the monster-mouth machine swept up everything in its path. The almighty-arm machine then deposited these loads, with a great deal of banging, clattering and thumping, into the back of another machine, which had a mammoth, up-turned shell on its back that seemed to be able to hold mountains of soil and ripped-up trees.

The watching animals trembled and sweated, even though the rain was painfully cold and wet. Once the monster's shell was full of soil and rocks and trees, the animals watched in trepidation as the machine then roared away, only to return about an hour later, to repeat the hideous process over and over again.

Eventually the monster-mouth machine had cleared about two thirds of the orange serpent's rectangular shape, having left out the lake, and it was now nearing the edge of the forest, and where the animals quivered and pressed together in fear and disbelief. The groaning and screeching noises it made, as it flattened the mud and slashed, wrestled and ripped up the trees, roots and plants (and no doubt, also some small, terrified animals such as moles, mice and insects) were indescribably horrible.

Those few animals who had stayed to watch, now realised it was time to leave the forest. The machines and destruction were getting too close.

So with heavy and fearful hearts beating with dread, dismay and despair, most of the last animals ran or walked or crawled or flew away, out of the forest and across the fields - to find somewhere to shelter from the obliteration of their homes and the eternal rain.

~~~~~~~~
~~~~~~~~

~ Chapter 9: Terrible Things ~

The crow, who as you might remember, was thought by many to have some of the glossiest and blackest feathers of all birds, and was almost always regarded as bossy and noisy but certainly clever, was often to be seen right at the very tops of trees, where he would sit and watch for miles across the countryside. He saw a lot of things and these things made him wonder, and over many seasons, helped to make him wiser.

He watched the unfolding drama beneath him in the little kidney-shaped forest and connecting fields. He watched as the animals, his acquaintances who had always lived in the little forest, had to leave in a hurry, crying and panicking, streaming off in all directions across

the fields and away from their homes in the
forest.

He watched as some of them fled into
hedgerows, holes, bushes, ditches and banks,
while others retreated further to distant little
forests, similar to this one, and tried to integrate
into the animal communities already living there,
which were already crowded.

He watched as the bulldozer, loader, trucks,
tools and humans systematically destroyed the
field below him and part of the forest. He
watched as a truck with an oblong tank on its
back, stretched out a long, snaking hose and
sucked away all that had once been the lake
where animals had lived and drank life-giving
water.

He watched as the young humans who had tried
to stop the annihilation of the forest and field,

returned one day with more young humans and some adult humans. He watched as they stood unwaveringly in the way of the worker humans and their enormous machines. He watched as they argued relentlessly for their case; he watched as the worker humans got angry and called the police; he watched as the young humans and their friends shouted and cried as they were forced to leave, and some were led away into police vans.

He watched as some of the worker humans stood in the centre of the field they had brutally demolished, talking and laughing. Snippets of their conversation floated up in the wind to the crow, like broken wings. He heard them say something about "environmental impact assessment" and "nothing's endangered, so it doesn't matter", then laugh when someone else said "those kids, interfering little whatchamacallits, threatened to go to the newspapers".

Of course, as clever as the crow was, he couldn't understand human language, so the words simply fluttered past him and mingled with the leaves and dust in the wind. What he didn't know was that the young humans and their friends had tirelessly been contacting the local newspapers, the council, and their parliamentary representatives. What the crow couldn't know was, despite all their efforts, unfortunately the building works had been allowed to continue this time.

He watched in the coming days and months as the bulldozer and the humans and their other machines ploughed, plundered and pillaged, and then roughly smoothed over the mud to prepare for the messy, eratic and loud process of building large abodes for other humans to come and live in.

He watched as a colossal, towering crane with an impossibly long and enormous arm, which reached higher than some trees and certainly higher than the crow's favourite perch, and large cubes of bricks and pyramidal roof trusses and enormous concrete mixing trucks came and jostled and joggled and bashed and bombarded, and somehow concocted buildings out of their midst.

He watched as humans with tools entered the forest below him and cut and slashed away more trees and bushes, then laid convoluted and meandering concrete tracks to prepare for other humans to walk along and ride their bicycles on and enjoy.

He watched as some of the smaller animals eventually crept back carefully into what was left of the forest, and tried to live there despite the constant breaching of their peace, while the building works continued for many seasons.

Finally the crow watched as the new houses with pristine fawn-coloured walls and perfectly manicured green lawns welcomed more humans into this place. He watched as furniture removal trucks drove up and unloaded mountains of furniture into the new houses for the humans' comfort.

And he watched as the humans who now lived there, who had inadvertently claimed this land and forest as their own, drove their cars and bicycles and baby strollers and scooters around the newly laid roads which had once been fields, meadows and forests; he watched as they played and laughed and fought and cried and grew up;

he watched as they completely took over without seeming to consider for one moment what had happened to the animals who had lived there.

And as the crow watched the humans' unstoppable "progress" over many years, he hoped that this kind of tragedy would *not* be repeated too often in other fields, meadows and forests.

But somehow he knew this was wishful thinking. Unless, like the young humans he had witnessed trying to stand up for the animals in this forest, more humans joined the side of the animals and the natural world.

~~~~~~~~
~~~~~~~~

~ This is the end of the story, but not of the book ~

Read the next few pages to find out **who the story's animal characters are named to honour and why**, *and to get further information and website links for research and discussion, ideas to explore further, and guidance on what you can do to help animals and the environment.*

~ Epilogue: Character Names and Websites ~

There is a growing movement across the Earth where ordinary children, teenagers and adults are standing up for their basic human rights and animals' rights, to clean air, water and land; and protesting against the mining, logging and other corporations whose agenda it seems is to pursue profits regardless of the cost to environmental, animal and human health.

In celebration of this, **some animals in this story are in honour of, and in solidarity with individual/groups of activists, defenders, indigenous tribes, and places where ordinary people came together and took action for their rights.** These people haven't always won these environmental conflicts, but they have been loyal and brave, even in the face of danger.

There are of course many more battles than those listed below and most of these crusades continue. They exist to secure hope for your and my futures as much as for saving what's left now, and they would be stronger with everyone's support.

See the following list. I urge you to look at the websites with a parent/carer/teacher or other responsible adult, because some of the material in the websites may be difficult to understand or process.

Note that some of these website links may disappear or change, but I update them occasionally. Alternatively, please search for the information in a search engine.

<u>List of main characters, who they honour, and website links for further information [updated November 2025]</u>

Balcombe the Badger – to honour Balcombe anti-drilling groups, Sussex, UK. For more info, see: https://www.facebook.com/FrackFreeSussex/ [link is active; last accessed Nov 9, 2025].

Barton the Badger – to honour Barton Moss anti-fracking protection camps and groups, Salford, Manchester, UK. For more info, see: https://www.facebook.com/BartonMoss/ [link is no longer active].

Try this one instead - it covers fracking in general and the environmental destruction it causes, with focus on the UK: https://friendsoftheearth.uk/climate-change/fracking [link is active; last accessed Nov 9, 2025].

Bentley the Bat – to honour Bentley anti-drilling blockade communities, New South Wales, Australia. For more info, see: http://csgfreenorthernrivers.org/ [link is no longer active].

http://www.lockthegate.org.au/ [link is active; last accessed Nov 9, 2025].

Dakota the Deer – to honour water protectors and activists at Standing Rock against Dakota Access Pipeline (DAPL), USA. For more info, see: http://www.ienearth.org/stand-with-standing-rock-no-dapl/ [link is no longer active]. https://www.nodaplarchive.com/ [link is active; last accessed Nov 9, 2025].

Flint the Fox – to honour the community affected by polluted water supplies in Flint, Michigan, USA. For more info, see: http://michaelmoore.com/10FactsOnFlint/ [link is no longer active].

Try this one instead: https://www.nrdc.org/stories/flint-water-crisis-everything-you-need-know [July 1, 2025] [link is active; last accessed Nov 9, 2025].

Moxat the Muntjac Deer – to honour the Moxatetéu [Moxihatetea] people, part of the Yanomami people, who are some of the last uncontacted tribes of Brazil and Venezuela. For more info, see: http://www.independent.co.uk/news/world/americas/in-2011-there-are-100-uncontacted-tribes-worldwide-2205746.html [Feb 6, 2011] [link is active; last accessed Nov 9, 2025].

http://www.survivalinternational.org/tribes/yanomami [link is active; last accessed Nov 9, 2025].

Rima the Rabbit – to honour Ridhima Pandey, a 9 year old girl who filed a legal case with the National Green Tribunal (NGT) against the Indian government for failing to protect the environment. For more info, see: http://www.independent.co.uk/environment/nine-ridhima-pandey-court-case-indian-government-climate-change-uttarakhand-a7661971.html [April 1, 2017] [link is active; last accessed Nov 9, 2025]. https://yourstory.com/2017/04/girl-petition-center-climate/ [April 5, 2017] [link is active; last accessed Nov 9, 2025].

Newly added: Ridhima Pandey received the Young Naturalist Award in 2020: https://sanctuarynaturefoundation.org/award/ridhima-pandey [link is active; last accessed Nov 9, 2025].

Tezcat the Tawny Owl – to honour Xiuhtezcatl Martinez, teenage environmental activist and Youth Director of Earth Guardians [until 2019]; also one of 21 youths who filed a legal case against the USA government and various fossil fuel groups for failing to protect the environment (Juliana vs United States, 2015).

For more info, see:
http://www.earthguardians.org/xiuhtezcatl [link is no longer active].
https://www.ourchildrenstrust.org/us/federal-lawsuit/ [link is no longer active].

Try this one instead - Xiuhtezcatl, now known as X, is an environmental activist and acclaimed musician:
https://en.wikipedia.org/wiki/Xiuhtezcatl_Martinez [link is active; last accessed Nov 9, 2025].

Whanganui the Weasel – to honour the Whanganui River, North Island, New Zealand, which after a legal battle was eventually accorded the same legal status as people. Managed by the Whanganui iwi tribespeople. For more info, see:
https://www.theguardian.com/world/2017/mar/16/new-zealand-river-granted-same-legal-rights-as-human-being [Mar 16, 2017] [link is active; last accessed Nov 9, 2025].

~~~~~~~~

Note: This is a work of fiction. Some characters in the story are included to honour and in solidarity with certain activists, defenders, tribes or places. However any similarity between them, or anyone else, alive or dead, and the story characters' personalities, skills, language, actions,
~~~~~~~~

situations, locations or anything else are unintended and coincidental.

~~~~~~~~

<u>Here are some related environmental issues you may wish to find out more about:</u>

Crimes against Environmental Defenders: The Global Witness website covers cases of environmental crime and corruption across the world. Particularly sad are the cases of murdered environmental activists, land defenders and protectors. For more info, see:

https://www.globalwitness.org/en/campaigns/environmental-activists/defenders-earth/

Fracking: a controversial mining process which injects a mixture of water, sand and chemicals at high pressure into rocks deep below the surface, releasing gas and/or oil. Fracking is known to cause earthquakes, contaminated/polluted water, air and soil, and diseases/deaths of people and animals living nearby. Yet the fracking/mining companies and governments who allow it argue hard that it's safe and desirable. For more info, see:

http://frack-off.org.uk/
~~~~~~~~

http://www.greenpeace.org.uk/climate/fracking [link is no longer active]

Indigenous Tribes: Survival International is an information website covering the rights and abuses of tribal peoples across the world, including 'uncontacted tribes' who live mostly in Brazil, Peru and Venezuela, and who are sometimes interfered with or even murdered because they're in the way of the activities of logging / mining / agricultural / damming companies, cattle ranchers and drug traffickers. For more info, see:

http://www.survivalinternational.org/

Rights of Non-Human Persons: Some of the most intelligent mammals, such as chimpanzees, gorillas, whales, dolphins and elephants, are beginning to be accepted as having some more rights and in some cases have been accorded the legal status of 'non-human persons'. However this varies across countries and is not always universally applied, often because factory farms, circuses, zoos and animal-testing laboratories resist change. For more info, see:

https://ieet.org/index.php/IEET2/RNHP [link is no longer active]

https://www.nonhumanrights.org/

~~~~~~~~
~~~~~~~~

~ Research and Discussion Points ~

This animal story implies or suggests some questions and discussion points around environmental issues.

People, governments and corporations have a range of opinions on environmental issues, and there is not always one answer or solution to the problems. Unfortunately quite often these same people, government representatives and corporate executives don't always have full knowledge before they make judgements about these issues.

For example on the question of whether new housing developments should be allowed to occur in 'green', undeveloped or natural spaces (which are almost always habitats for wild animals), some people may argue that there are increasing numbers of people and they need houses to live in, so unfortunately green spaces must be used.

Still others will say that there are already close to enough houses for people – there are thousands of older or disused houses in towns and cities which could be fixed and lived in.

Many others are researching and developing alternative solutions, such as: 'tiny houses', houses out of recycled materials (for example, ship containers or discarded vehicle tyres), houses built to fit into nature more such as those designed for living 'off-grid' and sustainably, or prefabricated/modular apartments built on smaller pieces of land previously left to ruin.

It's important that we know as much as possible about various environmental issues, so that we can make objective and wise decisions to solve them. It's easy to deny there are problems, because that means we don't need to take any effort to research all aspects of the issue, and then to think and act differently.

But many times the truth of human destruction of our planet Earth is staring us in the face – the evidence of our interference is all around us, and it's time we did something about it.

Why not take the first step? I suggest you research and discuss all the different arguments as well as various potential solutions around at least one of the following four environmental crises:

- The concepts of 'global warming' and/or 'climate change', which are already affecting weather patterns by creating extra flooding and droughts, and thus affecting food production, loss of houses and land, and starvation.

- The concept of using fossil fuels to power many aspects of human lives (cars, making electricity for homes and factories, trucks transporting goods, fuel for jet planes, etc), the creation of pollution from fossil fuels, and the fact that fossil fuels will run out in just a few decades.

- The use of plastic and other packaging for almost every small and large product we buy, and the fact that plastic, other packaging and parts of products which are not broken down (eg. micro beads in toiletry products) are collecting in huge quantities as litter and waste on land but also in the oceans, are polluting the seas, and are maiming/killing sea animals.

- The commonly held belief by many people that humans are the most important inhabitants of planet Earth and that therefore we assume we have a right to take, plunder and use as much land, water, air and soil, as well as animals, to serve us and our needs; regardless of the fact that this attitude causes environmental problems and destruction of the only home we have – planet Earth.

~~~~~~~~~
~~~~~~~~~

~ What Can You Do To Help? ~

There are lots of ways for ordinary children, teenagers and adults like you and me to get involved and help, no matter how young or old you are, or where you live. Here are some suggestions to get you started:

<u>Become aware/educated about what's really going on</u>

This means you need to become an 'information warrior' and read a lot!

Like any warrior, you will need to become skilled at searching for buried information – but don't worry – the truth is there for us all; you must simply want to find it and make an effort to do so.

Know that sometimes what you are told or see in the mainstream media (these are the large and well-known newspapers, TV channels and internet websites) can be incomplete or inaccurate, because it's not always in the interests of those in control – local councils, governments, banks and corporations – to let ordinary people know everything.

Be aware that internet browsers are media channels, just like newspapers or TV channels, so they may selectively present certain 'official' or corporate websites for you at the top of search pages, rather than objectively offering you a mix of all websites including those which tell the real truth.

Ask questions - especially 'why?' Don't simply accept what you're reading or being told; instead think hard about it, look at it from different angles, and discuss and question everything.

<u>Be vigilant about what's going on</u>

This means keeping your eyes and ears open, and knowing what's happening around you, as any good warrior does. I don't mean in the playground; I mean in the wider world around you. Look out for changes in your local neighbourhood and the countryside, or news in local newspapers, for example.

Watch out for clues that building or development are about to happen. These could be things like: building notices being put up or developments announced in the media; big signboards suddenly appearing which advertise new housing estates, office blocks or shopping centres; or hoarding/fences being erected to cordon off building sites.

Keep an eye on what's happening in other parts of your country and in other countries too (sign up for online/email newsletters from environmental websites) – because sooner or later, if we're not aware or don't take action, these things might come to your country or local area too.

<u>Challenge what's going on</u>

Challenge your local council, your government and companies/corporations when they abuse their powers and decide to do things in the name of "development", "progress" or simply for profits, usually without much consideration for human or animal health or the effect on the environment.

Remember that, so often, despite the promised extra jobs, cheaper energy or more houses, these things can be very destructive to the environment, to animals and to humans, even if

Environmental Impact Assessments have been carried out.

Write to those in charge, contact them via their social media accounts like Facebook and Twitter, start and/or sign petitions, join activist groups, donate money or time, be part of protests, or contact the media (newspapers, magazines, radio, TV).

Basically do some or all of these things, whatever you're comfortable with and are able to do. The point is, don't do nothing!

It won't always be easy, however. Just like the young humans in the story who tried to stop the building works, not every challenge will be successful. But we have a duty for the future of the human race, the planet and all its inhabitants to challenge actions which harm us, and to let those in charge know that we oppose their actions and why.

<u>Tell everyone about what's going on</u>

Become an environmental ambassador and spokesperson. Discuss these issues whenever you can with family, friends, teachers, classmates, and anyone else who will listen.

Of course not everyone will care to listen, and some will argue with you. This is where it helps that you know your stuff and can argue back calmly, presenting the real facts.

No matter how small or local the issue, we need to make people aware that destructive changes are happening in the world which are often not beneficial for ordinary people, animals, the environment, and nor for the future of life on Earth.

Good luck, environmental warrior!

146

Animals in the Forest The Day Terrible Things Came is more than just a story.

It's also about talking, questioning and exploring environmental issues – those close to home (like housing developments) and those further afield (like loss of habitats and mass extinctions).

To aid this exciting process of teaching and learning, supplementary WonderWorksheets are available from KathrynRoseNewey.com.

WonderWorksheets are essentially English/Literacy and Environmental worksheets, with lots of comprehension-style questions, discussion ideas and fiction/non-fiction writing tasks, as well as suggested research topics, based around the story.

They aim to encourage talking, reading, writing, questioning and exploring ideas. Perfect for parents, teachers, private tutors, homeschoolers, clubs, etc.

If you enjoyed this book and/or the WonderWorksheets, please share your thoughts on social media (#animalsintheforest) or write a review at amazon, at the website you obtained them, or at KathrynRoseNewey.com.

Thank you!